19

1)9

)20

Silver Dolphins

BROKEN PROMISES

C:

*To Alistair, William, Tim and Antonia for putting up with
late dinners and broken plates*

First published in paperback by HarperCollins *Children's Books* in 2009

HarperCollins *Children's Books* is a division of HarperCollins *Publishers* Ltd,
77-85 Fulham Palace Road, Hammersmith, London W6 8JB.

Visit our website at: www.harpercollins.co.uk

1 3 5 7 9 10 8 6 4 2
ISBN-13: 978-0-00-730972-6

Text copyright © Julie Sykes 2009
Cover illustrations copyright © Andrew Farley 2009

The author asserts the moral right to be identified
as the author of the work.

A CIP catalogue record for this title is available from the British Library.
All rights reserved.

Printed and bound in England by Clays Ltd, St Ives plc

Mixed Sources
Product group from well-managed
forests and other controlled sources
www.fsc.org Cert no. SW-COC-1806
© 1996 Forest Stewardship Council
FSC

FSC is a non-profit international organisation established to promote the
responsible management of the world's forests. Products carrying the FSC
label are independently certified to assure consumers that they come
from forests that are managed to meet the social, economic and
ecological needs of present and future generations.

Find out more about HarperCollins and the environment at
www.harpercollins.co.uk/green

by Summer Waters

Silver Dolphins

BROKEN PROMISES

HarperCollins *Children's Books*

Prologue

The summer storm came from nowhere. Rain beat down and the squalling wind whipped up the waves until they were higher than houses. Out at sea, thirty dolphins followed their leader as he dived underwater. It was a struggle to swim in the churning ocean as they headed for the seabed. Fighting tired muscles, the dolphins battled on until gradually, the ocean's mighty force lessened. At last the pod reached the bottom where all was calm and dark. For a while they chatted excitedly in whistles and clicks. Then, one by one they began to rest, the youngest first, followed by the adults, swimming together in a slow lazy circle.

Soon only two dolphins were properly awake; Star, a pretty dolphin with dark friendly eyes and Spirit, the leader.

"That was unexpected," whispered Star, nuzzling at Spirit affectionately.

Spirit nuzzled his wife back.

"There is more to come," he clicked. "I sense stormy times ahead for our Silver Dolphins."

"Surely not," squeaked Star, alarmed.

"Hush," soothed Spirit. "The Silver Dolphins will ride out the storm just as we do now."

Star's eyes were anxious.

"It won't be easy for them," she clicked.

"Being a Silver Dolphin is never easy," Spirit replied. "But the struggle is worthwhile."

"Can we help them?" asked Star.

"The Silver Dolphins must find their own way," said Spirit calmly. "But yes, we will be with them on their journey."

Chapter One

Antonia Lee trod water, staring around at the empty sea. Where was everyone hiding? Movement over by the rocks caught her eye. Antonia squinted into the sunlight. Was that Cai? She thought she could see his curly brown hair sticking over the top of the rock. Antonia turned her back, pretending she

hadn't noticed him. Casually she swam in the opposite direction, then diving down, she doubled back underwater. In one hand she trailed a long piece of crinkly brown seaweed. If she could sneak up on Cai and tag him then it would be his turn to be 'it'. She had almost reached the rocks when Cai broke cover. Like a rocket he shot past her, a huge grin on his face.

"Not 'it'," he called triumphantly.

Antonia grinned back as he disappeared. Cai hadn't been a Silver Dolphin for very long, but he was a quick learner. Already he was as at home in the water as their dolphin friends, Bubbles and Dream. Antonia swam on, her eyes searching for the dolphins. At last she saw them, hiding together in a kelp bed.

Antonia paddled through the kelp, parting it with her free hand. A school of tiny fish darted across her path, startling her. Taking advantage of her surprise, Dream and Bubbles made a dash for a new hiding place. The chase was on. Antonia pretended to follow Dream. Then, in a sudden change of direction, she lunged at Bubbles, tagging his tail with the seaweed.

"'It'!" she cried.

"No, you are," clicked Bubbles, flicking the seaweed back at her.

They played until the seaweed had almost disintegrated. Then, calling a truce, they floated on the sea's surface, enjoying the warmth of the sun on their faces.

"We'd better get back," clicked Dream

eventually. "Dad's taking the pod fishing soon."

"Spoilsport," clicked Bubbles, flicking water at her.

Dream looked slightly cross until Cai flicked water back at Bubbles. That started a water fight with everyone splashing so hard they churned up the sea like a whirlpool.

"Enough," panted Antonia. "We have to go now. It's nearly tea time."

"Goodbye," said Bubbles, solemnly swimming forward as if to rub noses with her.

"Goodbye... BUBBLES!" she shrieked as, catching her unawares, he doused her with water.

Bubbles clicked a laugh. "See you soon, Silver Dolphin," he called, keeping a safe distance away.

"I'll get you for that," Antonia laughed back.

She waited for Cai to finish saying goodbye to Dream, then rubbed noses with the older dolphin. The dolphins swam out to sea, leaping in and out of the water, their silver bodies curving like half-moons. Antonia and Cai headed in the opposite direction, swimming in companionable silence until Antonia suddenly exclaimed, "We've forgotten the rubbish."

She flushed guiltily, but Cai just laughed.

"Well remembered," he said placidly.

Somersaulting neatly they swam back to the rocks to collect their bundle: several crisp packets, an old shoe and two polystyrene cups all wrapped up in a split carrier bag.

"What would have happened if we'd left this behind?" Antonia idly wondered. "Do you think Spirit would have been cross?"

"No," said Cai. "Spirit knows we're not perfect. Everyone makes mistakes. We might not have been allowed to play with Bubbles and Dream for a bit, though."

"We shouldn't make mistakes," said Antonia emphatically.

"Everyone does," said Cai wisely. "Don't be too hard on us just because we're Silver Dolphins."

Antonia lightly touched the silver dolphin charm hanging round her neck. As Silver Dolphins, Antonia and Cai were guardians of the sea. Whenever Spirit called for their help a special magic let them swim like dolphins so they could sort the problem out.   Silver Dolphin magic was very rare. Antonia and Cai only knew one other person who had it: Claudia, Cai's great-aunt. She had been a Silver Dolphin before deciding that she was too old to do the job properly. Now she ran a marine conservation charity called Sea Watch instead.

They parted company at Claudia's beach.

"I'll take the rubbish," said Cai. "It can go in the Sea Watch bins. Where did you leave your shoes?"

"Gull Bay," said Antonia. It was her favourite beach after Claudia's because not many tourists knew about it. "See you tomorrow then."

"See you," said Cai.

Antonia swam on. She was enjoying every minute of the school holidays. So far, she'd spent most of it at Sea Watch with Cai. Leaping in and out of the water Antonia relished her freedom. Gull Bay was quiet with only a handful of people left on the beach. Antonia swam until she could see the seabed then, standing up, she waded ashore. Water poured from her clothes, leaving them as dry as if she'd been playing in the sun. Only her hair was slightly damp. Her sandals were where she'd left them, at the far end of the beach. Ramming her feet into them, Antonia padded across the sand.

She was almost home when someone called her name. Turning, Antonia saw her other best friend, Sophie, running towards her. As usual, Sophie was carrying her sketch book.

"Hi, I can't believe we haven't seen each other since the holidays started," panted Sophie, catching Antonia up.

"Me neither," said Antonia guiltily. "What have you been up to?"

"Helping Dad and drawing mostly. I'm getting really good at cats. A lady in one of Dad's classes has commissioned me to paint her cat for her. She's going to send me a photograph to copy from when she gets home."

"Well done! That's brilliant news!" Antonia exclaimed.

Sophie's dad was an artist and in the summer he ran art classes for the tourists.

Sophie was very good at art too and her latest project was sketching and painting cats. And now someone was paying her for it!

They reached the end of the road.

"Let's do something together soon," said Sophie.

"Definitely," Antonia agreed. "I'll ring you."

Antonia ran the rest of the way home. Pushing open the front door, she could hear lots of banging upstairs.

"Mum?" she called out.

"Up here, darling," Mum shouted back. "Come and give me a hand."

Antonia went upstairs and found her mother slowly backing out of the cupboard on the landing.

"Help me with this," she panted.

Antonia reached out and took some of the weight of the large bin bag her mother was carrying.

"What is it?" she asked.

"The put-you-up and the airbed," said Mum. "Aunty Sue phoned today and arranged for Abi and Ella to come and stay for a week."

"Great," said Antonia enthusiastically. She hadn't seen her cousins since Christmas and it would be fun to have them to stay. Abi was eleven, a whole year older than Antonia, but they got on really well. Jessica, Antonia's seven-year-old sister, and Ella, also seven, were good friends too.

"I can take Abi to Sea Watch. She'll love it. When are they coming?"

"Wednesday."

"But that's the day after tomorrow," Antonia squeaked.

"That's why I'm getting the beds out to air," said Mum, laughing.

"It's going to be such fun," said Antonia happily. "Which bed is Abi having? I'll put it straight in my room."

Chapter Two

The following morning, there was a new girl at Sea Watch. She seemed quite at home sitting at the large table next to Eleanor, Emily and Oliver, who were telling her about the Sea Watch litter-picking event scheduled for Saturday.

"Hi, everyone," said Antonia, including the

new girl in her greeting. "Where's Cai?"

"He's outside feeding Tilly," said Emily.

Tilly, an abandoned seal pup rescued by Claudia, had been at Sea Watch for a few days and was already making good progress.

"This is Hannah," Emily added. "Her mum's working in the area so she'll be here for a couple of weeks."

Hannah smiled at Antonia. She was pale and thin with long red hair. She would have seemed fragile, had it not been for her piercing grey eyes. Antonia was transfixed. She couldn't stop staring at Hannah. A strong feeling swept over her. Hannah was no ordinary girl. Antonia sensed there was something special about her. It was as if...

Hannah stared back with open curiosity and Antonia pulled herself together. What was wrong with her? Of course there wasn't anything special about Hannah. Only last week, she'd suspected her own sister of being a Silver Dolphin and she'd been completely wrong about that! Quickly she headed outside to find Cai.

The seal pup had just finished her bottle and was nosing at Cai's hand for more. Antonia laughed as Cai held the empty bottle out of her reach, saying, "You'll get wind if you suck on that."

"Do you want any help cleaning out her pen?" asked Antonia.

"Yes please," said Cai. "Guess what? Aunty Claudia's found a builder. He's going to start

work on the deepwater pool in a couple of weeks."

"That's fantastic," said Antonia. A deepwater pool was just what Sea Watch needed to rehabilitate seabirds and marine animals, like Tilly.

The seal pup followed Antonia and Cai as they tidied up her pen, occasionally nudging their feet with her shiny nose. She reminded Antonia of a puppy, but she knew better than to treat her like one. It was important to handle wild animals as little as possible or they became too tame to release back into the wild. They were almost finished when a familiar sensation swept over Antonia. Spirit was about to call. She stood still, listening for his voice in her head.

Silver Dolphin, come quickly.

Spirit, I hear your call.

Antonia didn't speak, but thought the words. Cai was only able to communicate with Spirit through his silver dolphin charm and didn't know about her telepathy. A few seconds later, both Antonia's dolphin necklace and the dolphin badge pinned to Cai's T-shirt began to vibrate. Both charms thrashed wildly then they broke into a high-pitched whistle.

"Silver Dolphin, come quickly."

"Spirit, I hear your call," said Cai.

He sprinted out of the seal pen, pulling off his rubber gloves and quickly locking the door after Antonia followed him out.

Together they ran for the beach, vaulting

the tiny gate and heading for the Sea Watch boat where they stopped to leave their shoes. Antonia touched her charm, concerned by how fast the dolphin's tail was beating. Spirit needed them urgently. As she splashed into the sea she heard a whispering noise in her head. Puzzled, Antonia slowed, trying to work out what it was. Her silver dolphin charm beat more wildly. There was no time to solve the mystery. Ignoring the whispering noise, Antonia threw herself into the water.

The moment her legs melded together like a tail she swam. She didn't wait for Cai, and used her powerful Silver Dolphin magic to propel her through the water, her streamlined body arching in and out of the sea like a real dolphin, only much faster. She swam almost to the headland to the west of Sandy Bay beach before she felt vibrations in the water. Hoping they were caused by Spirit, Antonia swam on. At last she saw his silvery head bobbing in the sea near the cliffs. Antonia raced over.

"Hurry, Silver Dolphin," Spirit clicked, his eyes concerned. "A bird's in trouble on the cliffs."

Antonia scanned the cliffs, searching for the unfortunate bird. There it was – about two metres up, perched on a ledge, a large seagull with untidy feathers. Its head bobbed back and forth and its body heaved as if it was choking. What was that hanging from its beak? Antonia couldn't quite make it out. She swam towards the cliff face. She'd never been

rock climbing before, but luckily the cliff was craggy with plenty of hand and footholds. Antonia reached up and placed her hand on a jutting-out piece of rock. It was wet and slippery, but big enough for her to wrap both hands round it to pull herself out of the water. Her knees grazed against rock and she winced as her feet found their own footholds. She looked up, searching for the next hand hold and found one above her head and another one to the right. Reaching up, she pulled herself higher. The climb wasn't difficult and Antonia felt safe, knowing that if she fell it was only a short drop into the sea.

The bird was making a horrible noise. Antonia climbed faster. She called out in a soothing voice as she drew nearer, but the bird was too distressed to notice. Hauling herself on to the ledge, Antonia saw it was choking on the plastic top of a yoghurt pot. Antonia shuffled her feet until she was balanced. There wasn't much room on the ledge and she didn't want to slip off. How best to help the bird? Tentatively she held out her hand. The bird hardly noticed as it carried on gagging. Antonia knew, from some basic first-aid training at school, that when someone was choking and couldn't breathe you had to act fast. A slap on the back was often enough to remove the thing they were choking on, or there was a more complicated manoeuvre that involved putting your arms round them and squeezing. The gull was definitely having problems breathing. Antonia leant forward.

Stroking its head with her left hand, she gently tried freeing the yoghurt pot lid from its beak with her right. The lid shifted a little, then wouldn't move any further.

"Steady," crooned Antonia, as the bird began to stagger forward.

She tried pulling at the plastic again, but it wouldn't budge. The bird made a funny gurgling sound in its throat. Desperate to stop it from suffocating, Antonia gently tapped it on the back between the wings. The bird coughed, staggered forward, then fell on its side. Antonia stared at it in disbelief. It looked dead. Had she killed it?

"Please be alive."

Carefully she lifted the gull up, as if by doing so everything would suddenly be all right. Its head flopped to one side. The yoghurt pot lid hung from its open beak. Antonia's brain felt like rush hour. Thoughts zoomed back and forth, making her giddy. *You killed it. No I didn't. You did, it was your fault. But how? I was trying to save it.*

Silver Dolphin.

Spirit's voice broke into the chaos in her head.

It's not your fault.

I killed it.

No. You answered the call. You did your best.

Antonia didn't feel like she'd done her best. She laid the bird back on the ledge, stroking its head and smoothing down its feathers.

"I'm sorry."

The bird stared back at her with lifeless

eyes. Sadly, Antonia looked at the sea. Was it safe to dive from here or should she climb back down? From the water, three faces stared up at her. Antonia did a double take. There was Spirit and that was Cai, so who was treading water next to him? Antonia blinked as she stared at the pale skinny girl in the water. There was no mistaking that bright red hair. It was Hannah.

Chapter Three

Hannah was a Silver Dolphin! Antonia's stomach plummeted. At once she had a sudden desire to climb up the cliff face and escape from everyone. It was bad enough failing in front of Spirit and Cai, but to do it in front of new girl Hannah was mortifying! It made Antonia's skin prickle. But the trouble with running

away was that at some point you had to come back. Taking a deep breath to give her courage, Antonia began to climb back down the cliff. When she finally splashed into the sea, Cai and Hannah swam over to meet her. They were so sympathetic it made her feel worse.

"At least you reached it in time," said Cai, squeezing her hand. "I was miles behind. When I realised Hannah was a Silver Dolphin, I hung back to show her where to go."

"Bad luck with the bird," said Hannah. "A similar thing happened to me once. That was a seagull too and it almost died."

"This isn't your first time as a Silver Dolphin?" Antonia was surprised.

With a wide smile, Hannah pulled a

necklace from under her T-shirt. A silver dolphin charm hung from it.

"I've been a Silver Dolphin since I was ten. I'm eleven now."

"So... how did you know? Do you have someone like Claudia? She was a Silver Dolphin once. She gave me my dolphin necklace and Cai his badge."

"Yes, her name's Kathleen. She's a friend of Mum's. She's marvellous with animals. She's always got a collection of sick and injured pets and wildlife. She cares for them in her house, even though it's only tiny."

"Do you know Spirit?"

Hannah shook her head. "But Vision does. He's the leader of our dolphin pod."

"I know Vision well," Spirit agreed. "I must

remember to thank him for letting us borrow his Silver Dolphin."

Antonia felt a sharp pang of jealousy and, even though she quickly squashed it, she couldn't quite meet Hannah's eye when she said, "It's great to have you here."

"Definitely," clicked Cai enthusiastically. "There's always room for another Silver Dolphin."

Antonia could feel vibrations in the water. She turned and saw two small dolphins swimming towards them in graceful arcs.

"Bubbles and Dream," she whispered. Was there to be no end to her shame?

"Silver Dolphin," squeaked Bubbles, swimming straight to Antonia and greeting her with a gentle rub on the nose. His dark eyes held hers for a minute, then he rubbed her nose again before turning to Hannah and Cai.

"A new Silver Dolphin. How bubbly!"

Hannah laughed.

"Don't get too excited," she squeaked back. "I'm only here for a couple of weeks."

While Bubbles greeted Hannah and Cai properly, Dream swam alongside Antonia and touched her face with a flipper.

"You did your best," she clicked softly.

"Thanks." Antonia was grateful for Dream's kindness.

Bubbles was thrilled to meet a new Silver Dolphin and couldn't keep still. "Seaweed tag," he shouted, bobbing up and down in the water. "It'll be even more fun now."

Antonia wasn't in the mood to play. She didn't feel she deserved to have fun after the seagull had died.

"Not today," she clicked.

Cai hesitated, then said, "Next time. We've got to get back now."

Hannah nodded in agreement.

"Too bad," clicked Bubbles, flicking the sea with his tail. His disappointment made Antonia feel worse.

Don't be too hard on yourself.

Spirit's voice broke into her thoughts. Antonia looked up. His dark eyes held hers. Sadly she shook her head. If only it was that simple!

The dolphins swam with them to Claudia's beach before Spirit shepherded Bubbles and

Dream out to sea. The Silver Dolphins watched them go. When they were tiny dots on the horizon, they swam ashore.

"Kathleen would love Sea Watch," said Hannah suddenly. "Maybe she could set up something similar."

"Great idea," said Cai. "I bet Aunty Claudia would help her to get started. The more Sea Watches the better."

"You can't call it Sea Watch!" Antonia exclaimed. Her face reddened as Cai and Hannah stared at her. "I mean… you'd have to call it something else or people might get confused."

"I don't think they would," said Cai thoughtfully. "It would be a bit like the RSPCA. They have branches all over the country."

"I agree with Antonia," said Hannah surprisingly. "It would be better to call it something different, like, erm... I don't know, Beach Watch maybe."

Antonia gave Hannah a suspicious look, unsure if she was genuinely being nice or if she was making fun of her.

"How about Seaweed Watch," chuckled Cai, untangling a piece of seaweed from his leg as he waded towards the beach.

"Or Shell Watch," giggled Hannah, plucking an empty mussel shell from the seabed.

Antonia followed in silence, water cascading from her clothes as she made her way up the beach. Part of her wanted to join in, saying something silly like 'Waterfall

Watch' but her voice refused to make the words happen.

Claudia met them in the garden. Her eyes skipped over the giggling Hannah and Cai and rested on Antonia.

I failed.

Antonia thought the words before Claudia had time to ask.

It happens. Failure isn't a crime. Not trying is and before you ask, yes, I've failed lots of times. On one occasion it was very bad.

Claudia's sea-green eyes held a faraway look. Suddenly, Antonia remembered Bubbles telling her how one of their pod had got tangled in a fishing net and died because the Silver Dolphin was too far away to save her. Had that Silver Dolphin been Claudia? She

reached out for Claudia's hand and squeezed it. Claudia gave her hand a little squeeze back.

"Guess what?" said Cai, breathless with excitement.

"Antonia's lost her shoes?" asked Claudia, a twinkle in her eye.

Antonia grinned. It was becoming a bit of a joke that she kept leaving her shoes on the beach.

"No," said Cai. "Hannah's a Silver Dolphin."

"Oh, that!" said Claudia mischievously. "I had a suspicion she might be."

"She wants to set up a Sea Watch where she lives. Will you help her?" Cai rushed on.

Claudia laughed. "Of course I will. We'll talk about it later when I've got time to sit down with Hannah and discuss it properly. Right now I was hoping you three might clear out the shed for me. The builder needs to move it before he starts work on the deepwater pool."

Claudia suggested they lay everything housed in the shed on the lawn while she cleared a temporary space for it all in her garage.

"The car can stay outside," she said decisively.

Emptying the shed was great fun. It was chock-full with all sorts of interesting things, including lots of old boat bits.

"What's this?" asked Cai, pulling an intriguing-looking object out of a cardboard box labelled 'Boat Safety'. He turned it over and it rattled in his hand.

"It's a container," said Antonia. "That bit unscrews."

She leant closer, wanting to know what was inside.

"Antonia," bellowed a voice.

At first Antonia ignored it, but when the person kept on shouting she hung out of the shed to see what they wanted. Emily was standing at the other end of the garden waving frantically.

"Quick! Your mum's on the phone."

Antonia stood half in and half out of the shed as Cai twisted the container's lid.

"It's moving, but it's very stiff."

"It'll probably be something totally boring inside," said Hannah.

Cai tapped the container against an

upturned bucket to try and release the lid.

"It might be money," he said hopefully.

Hannah giggled. "What, in a box labelled boat safety?"

"Antonia," bellowed Emily again.

Antonia sighed. "I'll be right back," she said.

"Hmph!" grunted Cai vaguely.

Crossly, Antonia ran up the garden to take the phone call. Trust Mum to insist on speaking to her right now. Why couldn't she have just left a message?

Chapter Four

"We're going into Trumouth," said Mum.

"That's nice," said Antonia, wondering why Mum had rung to tell her that.

"The airbed has a puncture. It wasn't terribly comfortable anyway so I'm going to replace it with another put-you-up."

"Can't you get one in Sandy Bay?"

"The shop that sells them is out of stock," Mum replied.

"Thanks for letting me know. I'll see you later," said Antonia dismissively.

"That's not what I meant," said Mum. "You're coming too."

"What! Why?" asked Antonia fiercely.

"It takes at least an hour to drive there. More if I get stuck in traffic. I don't want to be sat in a jam worrying about getting back for you."

"You don't have to worry about me. I'll be fine. There's plenty to do here at Sea Watch."

"I'm sorry, Antonia, but you're coming and that's final," said Mrs Lee. "I'll drive over and pick you up. Make sure you're ready to leave straightaway, please."

The line went dead. Mum had hung up. Antonia was so frustrated, she almost stamped her foot. She slammed the phone back in the receiver and went to tell Cai that she had to go. She could hear him and Hannah laughing together long before she reached the shed. Furiously she hurried over. It wasn't fair. Why did she have to miss out on the fun?

"Look at me," gasped Cai when she pulled open the door. "What do you think?"

The container he'd been trying to open lay abandoned on the floor.

"It was waterproof matches," said Cai, nodding at it. "But look what else we found. Does it suit me?"

Cai wore a bright yellow buoyancy jacket

with a tall inflatable flag attached to the shoulder. The flag, fluorescent orange and red, almost reached the shed's ceiling. Hannah was laughing so much there were tears in her eyes.

"Very nice," said Antonia, forcing a smile. "I came to tell you that I'm going. Mum's making me go shopping with her to Trumouth."

"Poor you," said Cai. He shrugged himself out of the buoyancy jacket. "It gets really busy there in the summer. Here, take this with you. Then your mum won't lose you in the crowds."

Hannah almost collapsed laughing.

"Thanks," said Antonia frostily. "But Hannah looks like she needs help more than I do."

Cai glanced at Antonia in surprise.

"Is your mum picking you up?" he asked, suddenly becoming serious.

Antonia nodded.

"I'll come and wait with you until she gets here."

"You don't have to."

"I do," said Cai.

The trip into town was a nightmare. The traffic was heavy and it took ages to get there. Jessica was a total pain, insisting Antonia played I Spy and other travel games that Antonia had long outgrown. Antonia reluctantly played along until Jessica started cheating and there was a squabble. Mum turned down the programme she'd been listening to on the radio. "There, there, girls! Antonia, calm down. Remember Jess is younger than you."

"She's old enough to know that cheating's not allowed," grumbled Antonia.

"Spoilsport! Don't play with me then. I don't care. I'll have Abi and Ella to play with soon," said Jessica.

"Jessica, that's not very nice," said Mum sternly. "I hope you'll all play together. I want you both to promise me that you won't squabble when your cousins arrive and that you'll look after them properly."

"I promise," said Jessica.

"Antonia?"

"Of course," said Antonia. "I can't wait to take Abi to Sea Watch."

Mum nodded, then added, "And if Abi doesn't want to go to Sea Watch, you'll find something she does want to do?"

"Yes," said Antonia. "But how could she not want to go to Sea Watch?"

Suddenly, Mum looked shifty. "It's been a while since you last saw Abi," she said carefully. "Just promise me you'll be a good host. Do the things Abi wants to do. It's only for a week."

Antonia stared at her mother in surprise.

"Promise?" Mum persisted.

"Yes," said Antonia, mystified. "I promise."

The conversation left Antonia feeling uncomfortable. What was Mum getting at? She turned it over in her mind until a very alarming thought struck her. What if Spirit called when her cousins came to stay? How would she get away without being missed? Antonia had promised Spirit always to answer his call. She'd also promised to keep the Silver Dolphins a secret. It would be difficult keeping all her promises.

When they returned from the shopping trip, Mum gave Antonia an armful of sheets and blankets and asked her to make up the two beds. Ella was sleeping in Jessica's room and after Antonia had made it, Jess piled the bed with cuddly toys so Ella wouldn't feel lonely at night. In her own room, Antonia emptied one of her drawers and cleared a space on the dressing table for Abi to put her hairbrush. She left a couple of books on the put-you-up for Abi to read: a unicorn one and a magical pony story. There was still half an hour left until tea, but Antonia couldn't settle. She wandered into the garden and stood staring out at the bay. What was Cai doing now? Would Hannah still be helping at Sea Watch? Hannah had said her mum often worked late, so she was allowed to stay out late too. It was weird knowing that Hannah was a Silver Dolphin. Remembering how Hannah had been there when she'd failed to save the choking seagull made Antonia turn hot with shame. She mustn't fail again. Next time she'd prove to Hannah that she was a good Silver Dolphin.

Chapter Five

Antonia woke with a sense of urgency. She was supposed to be doing something, but what was it? She lay with her eyes closed, sleepily trying to remember. The sensation grew stronger and at once Antonia realised what it meant. Spirit was about to call. She leapt out of bed and pulled on her clothes.

She finished dressing and tiptoed downstairs. Halfway down, her dolphin charm began to vibrate.

Spirit, I hear your call, thought Antonia as the charm let out a short whistle.

She clasped the charm in her hand, loving the way its metal body felt exactly like a real dolphin. In the kitchen, Antonia scribbled a hurried note to her parents telling them she'd gone for a walk. She quietly let herself out and was jogging down the street when the whispering in her head started. The first voice was Cai's telling Spirit he'd heard his call. It was followed by Hannah.

Spirit, I hear you. I'm on my way.

Antonia quickened her pace. As a very powerful Silver Dolphin only she could hear the other Silver Dolphins answering Spirit. They couldn't hear her. Even though she sensed that Spirit's call wasn't a life or death situation, Antonia was determined to reach him first. It was only when she got to Gull Bay that Antonia remembered her cousins were arriving that morning. They always came early as Aunty Sue liked to drive down overnight when there was less traffic. Antonia sat on the edge of the beach, an argument raging in her head as she pulled off her shoes and socks. The call wasn't urgent. Both Cai and Hannah were answering it. She wasn't really needed. Maybe she should go home and be there when her cousins arrived. But as a Silver Dolphin she had promised to answer the

call. Besides, after yesterday, she wanted to prove to Hannah she was a good Silver Dolphin.

Deciding she could answer the call and be home before her cousins got there, Antonia continued across the sand. She left her shoes and socks in a neat pile hidden by a rock, then dashed into the sea. The water was freezing, numbing her legs and making her gasp as she waded deeper. Finally she launched her body into the sea. At once the warmth returned as her legs melded together and began to work like a tail. Antonia whistled for joy, her body arching in and out of the water. But her happiness was short-lived. She swam out of Gull Bay and across Sandy Bay. Then, as she rounded the headland, Antonia saw three heads bobbing in the water. Both Cai and Hannah had beaten her to Spirit. Hannah was staying in a hotel very near Sea Watch, so didn't have as far to swim as she had, but still Antonia was annoyed. Cai waved and Antonia waved back, stretching her mouth into a smile that she didn't feel like making. She swam to Spirit first, rubbing her nose against his in greeting.

"Thank you for coming, Silver Dolphins," Spirit addressed them all. "I've found a container caught between some rocks. Can you take it ashore?"

Antonia nodded. This wasn't the first container from a ship that she'd helped ashore and it probably wouldn't be the last. Ships often lost things overboard. Sometimes

they even deliberately ditched things in the sea.

"There it is," clicked Spirit, pointing with his nose.

Antonia swam over to the rocks. The container was of bright green plastic with strong strips of tape wrapped round it to hold the lid on.

"Careful," warned Hannah, as Antonia swam closer. "It might contain something dangerous."

"I know that," said Antonia. She checked the surface of the container for holes and, finding none, dived under the water to examine the rest of it.

"It's not damaged," she declared as she surfaced. "And it doesn't have any hazard stickers either."

Cai gave it an experimental push and the container moved slightly.

"It should be easy enough to shift," he said. "We'll swim it back to Sea Watch. It's not far."

With everyone's help, they soon freed the container from the rocks. Antonia found herself wedged between Cai and Hannah as they swam it ashore.

We don't need her help, she thought sourly as they paddled towards Claudia's beach. She kept banging elbows with Hannah who was using one hand to swim and the other to push.

"Thank you, Silver Dolphins," clicked Spirit, when they were almost there.

He left them to rejoin his pod, his silver body shining in the early morning sun.

Wistfully Antonia watched him go. What were Bubbles and Dream doing now? It would have been fun to play with them both, especially after not feeling like it yesterday.

The Silver Dolphins swam until it was too shallow to do anything but paddle. As they rose from the sea the salty water poured from them, leaving their clothes instantly dry.

It was harder carrying the container on land. Cai and Hannah bagged the ends, leaving Antonia with the awkward position of middle. They staggered up the beach, stopping at the Sea Watch boat to collect their shoes.

"Oh!" exclaimed Hannah, suddenly realising that Antonia hadn't started from Claudia's beach. "Where are your shoes? How will you walk home?"

"Antonia keeps a spare pair here," said Cai, chuckling. "They're up at the house."

"Why don't you go on ahead then?" said Hannah kindly. "We can manage on our own if you leave the gate open, can't we, Cai?"

Antonia bristled. Who did Hannah think she was, giving her instructions?

"I'm fine," she said stiffly. "I'm used to managing without shoes."

"Well, if you're sure..." Hannah smiled in a friendly way. "You're so lucky having each other," she added. "I never realised how lonely being a Silver Dolphin can sometimes be until I met you. Kathleen rarely answers Vision's call these days. The water makes her rheumatism worse. It's great fun working in a group."

They carried the container to the Sea Watch building and left it outside.

"Aunty Claudia can sort it out from here," said Cai. "She'll probably ring her friend Jack the coastguard and get him to take it away."

They continued up to the house. The back door was ajar and a gorgeous smell drifted out from the kitchen.

"Mmm, bacon," Cai sniffed appreciatively.

He went inside and Antonia followed, but Hannah held back.

"Hello," said Claudia, waving a food slice at them. "Who wants a bacon sandwich for breakfast? Hannah? Don't stand outside then. Come on in."

"Thanks," beamed Hannah, her grey eyes lighting up. "Mum never bothers with breakfast and I hate eating in the hotel dining room on my own."

She stepped inside and sat down at the kitchen table.

"There you go." Claudia put a plate of sandwiches in the middle of the table. "Sit down, Antonia, before they go cold."

Antonia eyed the sandwiches longingly, but shook her head.

"I can't stop. My cousins are arriving this morning. I only came in to get my spare shoes."

Antonia's stomach grumbled noisily as she hurried home. She was starving hungry and hoped she hadn't missed her own breakfast. She made a quick detour down to Gull Bay to collect her shoes. Hopefully she could sneak

indoors without being seen, else there would be awkward questions to answer about why she'd gone out with two pairs of shoes! But as Antonia turned into the end of her road, she realised that shoes were the least of her problems. Aunty Sue's car was parked in the drive. Ella and Abi had arrived and she'd not been there to greet them!

Chapter Six

The adults were sitting at the kitchen table drinking cups of tea. There was no sign of Jessica and Ella, but Abi sat at the table with a bored expression on her face.

"Antonia, here you are at last," said Mum tightly. She was clearly furious, but Antonia was too shocked to notice. She glanced at

Abi, completely amazed at how much her cousin had changed since she'd last seen her. Abi was so grown up! Instead of her usual bunches she wore her blonde hair in a sleek bob. Her long fringe almost covered her blue eyes and she was wearing make-up.

"Back in a mo," said Mum lightly.

Gripping Antonia by the arm, she steered her out of the kitchen. In the hallway she lowered her voice to an angry whisper.

"And where have you been? You promised to be a good host, then you disappear on the very first day of your cousins' visit."

"I'm sorry," said Antonia. "It was such a lovely day. I felt like getting some fresh air."

"What was wrong with the fresh air in the

garden?" asked Mum. "I'm disappointed in you, Antonia. I thought you were looking forward to having Abi and Ella to stay."

"I am," squeaked Antonia. "I didn't realise they'd get here so early. It won't happen again, I promise."

"Make sure you keep your promise this time," said Mum. "Go and say a proper hello. Aunty Sue is almost ready to leave. Then you can take Abi up to your room and show her where to put her things."

Alone with Abi in her room, Antonia felt suddenly shy.

"I've cleared a space for you on my dressing table and there's a spare drawer for your clothes," she said hesitantly.

"Thanks," said Abi, unzipping her bag. She pulled out a jumble of clothes and began stacking them in the drawer. Antonia's eyes widened. How long was Abi planning to stay?

"I can empty another drawer if you need it," she offered.

"No worries," said Abi. "The rest of my stuff can stay in my case. I could do with a bit more room here, though." She went over to the dressing table and swept aside Antonia's things. Out of the bag came a ton of make-up, a hairbrush, three different body sprays, shampoo, conditioner and a huge bottle of shower gel. Wincing, Antonia moved her dolphin statue to the bedside table before it got broken.

"After breakfast, I thought we could go to Sea Watch," she said. "It's really cool there."

"Sea Watch?" questioned Abi. She picked up the books Antonia had left on the put-you-up, then dumped them back on Antonia's bed. "Thanks, but I read those ages ago."

"Sea Watch is a marine conservation charity. I go there to help. We're caring for a baby seal at the moment and we're planning a massive litter-picking event for this weekend."

"Litter-picking?" Abi raised her eyebrows. "And that's what you do for fun?"

Antonia looked at Abi uncertainly. Was she being teased? The old Abi would have loved going to Sea Watch.

"We can do something else if you'd rather," she said.

"No, Sea Watch is cool. Are we going now?"

"After breakfast," said Antonia.

"I don't eat breakfast," said Abi.

Mrs Lee encouraged Abi to eat a small slice of toast and drink some orange juice while Antonia wolfed down a bowl of cereal and several slices of toast.

"You don't have to go to Sea Watch if you'd rather not," said Mum, giving Antonia a hard stare. "I'm taking Jessica and Ella swimming this morning. You girls are welcome to come with us."

Abi gave a slight shudder.

"Thanks, Aunty Helen, but I'm not keen on swimming."

"You used to love it," said Mrs Lee, surprised.

"Yeah, well. I've grown up, I suppose. I start secondary school in September."

Antonia gave Abi a worried look. Some of her friends from Sea Watch started secondary school in September. She hoped Emily, Karen and Eleanor weren't going to change as suddenly as Abi had.

By the time Antonia and Abi arrived at Sea Watch, Hannah and Cai had finished feeding Tilly and freshening up her pen. Antonia tried not to mind that she'd missed out on the fun. A spark of the old Abi returned when she saw the seal.

"Poor little thing," she exclaimed. "Why is she so skinny?"

"She lost her mum," said Cai.

"Can I hold her?" Abi pushed a finger through the netting and wiggled it.

"Careful she doesn't bite you. We handle the wild animals as little as possible," said Cai, coming out of the pen with Hannah and locking the door. "It's not good for them if they become too tame."

"Oh!" Abi was disappointed. "So what else is there to do?"

"Lots of things," said Antonia quickly. "Let's go and find Claudia. She's never short of jobs."

Claudia was inside the Sea Watch building, putting together some mysterious-looking blue panels.

"What's that for?" asked Antonia.

"They're display boards," said Claudia, pushing her curly brown hair away from her face. "They're for the litter-picking event on Saturday. I'm going to put up some posters and information on the terrible effects that litter pollution has on the marine life. Even if people don't join in with the event the posters will hopefully make them think about disposing of their rubbish more carefully."

"Can we help put them together?" asked Cai.

"Antonia can help me," said Claudia. "Please could the rest of you start making up the litter-picking packs? Each volunteer will be given a pair of disposable gloves, a black sack for rubbish, a green one for

recycling, a carton of juice and some biscuits in a recyclable box. I'm expecting around fifty volunteers. You'll find everything you need over there. Oh good, here's Emily and Oliver. Get them to help you."

Claudia winked at Antonia as Cai and Hannah took Abi off to start their task.

"There are two more panels in the garage. Will you help me get them?" she asked.

"Of course," said Antonia, following Claudia outside.

"How's it going with Abi?" asked Claudia as they walked to the garage.

"Fine," said Antonia.

"Really? Abi seems uncomfortable. I'm getting the impression that she feels out of place and bored."

Antonia forced a smile. She could hide her thoughts and moods from Claudia if she wanted to, but what was the point?

"You're right. It's not fine," she admitted. "Abi's changed since I saw her at Christmas. She's into different things."

"You don't have to come to Sea Watch every day if Abi doesn't want to," said Claudia. "You could take a holiday."

Antonia said nothing as she remembered her promise to Mum. She twisted a strand of her long blonde hair round a finger. How could she manage to stay away from Sea Watch for a whole week? And what about the Silver Dolphins? It would be really difficult to answer the call if she was looking after Abi on her own.

"You can take a holiday from the Silver Dolphins too."

Antonia jumped in surprise. She'd been unaware that Claudia had tuned in to her thoughts and her suggestion shocked Antonia.

"I can't ignore Spirit's call," she said emphatically. "I promised I'd always answer him."

"There are three of you now. Cai and Hannah can manage on their own."

Antonia remained silent. Not answering Spirit's call would be impossible. Knowing Hannah was a Silver Dolphin only made it worse. Antonia wanted to prove to Hannah that she didn't usually make mistakes.

"Promise me you'll think about it," said Claudia calmly.

Reluctantly Antonia nodded. So many promises! How on earth could she keep them all?

Chapter Seven

That evening over tea, Mum made an announcement.

"I'm taking you girls out tomorrow. We're going to spend the day at Oak Manor."

"The theme park?" Abi stopped playing with her food and looked interested.

"Wicked!" squealed Jessica and Ella.

"What, all day?" asked Antonia, putting down her knife and fork.

"Well, of course all day," said Mum. "It's a big place."

Antonia had never been to Oak Manor, but she'd heard the rides were brilliant. It was the zoo part she wasn't keen on. The zoo had tigers and a golden eagle. Antonia didn't agree with such magnificent wild animals being penned up. But her main reason for not wanting to go to Oak Manor was that it was inland. How would she answer Spirit if he called while she was there?

"Can't we go to The Lakes instead?"

The Lakes were only down the road and right near a beach.

"Boring," sung Jessica. "We can go to The

Lakes any time. Not that I'd want to. The rides are so babyish."

Mum gave Antonia one of her looks. "We're going to Oak Manor," she said firmly. "It's all arranged. I've invited Sophie along too."

That was a nice surprise. Antonia smiled at Mum gratefully. It would be fun to spend the day with Sophie. And having her around might make things easier with Abi. Looking after her cousin was hard work. Abi had been bored at Sea Watch and made her boredom embarrassingly clear. Claudia offered to take Cai, Antonia, Abi and Hannah surfing after Sea Watch had closed for the day, but Abi hadn't wanted to join in with that either.

"I don't do water," she said.

Sophie would know the right things to say to Abi. She got along with everyone. Helping out at her dad's art classes had given her lots of practice as she had to be friendly to all sorts of people.

After tea, Antonia went into the garden to look at Sandy Bay. The sky was blue and the sea sparkled like millions of tiny sapphires in the evening sunlight. Antonia longed to be in the water, surfing with Cai and Hannah, or swimming with her dolphins. Her fingers strayed to her silver dolphin charm. Its soft body juddered slightly to her touch. Antonia stood very still. Was Spirit about to call? She waited, but there was no sense of being needed. She smiled to herself. She'd noticed her charm reacted to her touch sometimes; it was as if Spirit was telling her that all was well. Feeling happier, Antonia went indoors to join Abi, who was slumped in front of the television watching one of the soaps.

Oak Manor was a huge success. Everyone had a great time, except for Antonia. She wanted to enjoy herself. The rides were spectacular, but nothing could possibly compare with the thrill of swimming with the dolphins. Antonia spent the day wondering if Spirit would call and worrying about how she would answer him if he did. Although she had promised to think about taking a holiday from the Silver Dolphins, Antonia didn't give it any serious thought. If Spirit needed her she knew she would go to him. Knowing that Hannah was around made things worse, not better. Hannah worried Antonia. She seemed so competent. It was hard to believe that she ever made mistakes. What if after the seagull disaster Hannah thought Antonia wasn't a good Silver Dolphin?

To Antonia's relief, Abi got on fantastically well with Sophie. They had lots of things in common, including a love of jewellery-making. Abi was more animated when talking to Sophie than Antonia had seen her since she'd arrived.

By mid-afternoon the theme park was packed. People were queuing for over an hour to go on the rides so Mrs Lee decided it was time to go home. Antonia could hardly hide her relief. Then, as they drove into Sandy Bay, a familiar sensation swept over her. Spirit was

about to call. Antonia willed her mother to drive faster but Mrs Lee was keeping to the thirty-mile-an-hour limit.

"Could I go to Sea Watch for a bit when we get home?" asked Antonia impatiently. "I won't be long. There's something I need to finish before the litter-pick this weekend."

"Can't it wait?" asked Mrs Lee, flicking the indicator down as she prepared to turn into Sophie's road.

Softly Antonia's charm began to vibrate. She was desperate to answer it. "It won't take long," she pleaded.

Sophie leant forward between the seats. "Abi can come home with me if she likes, Mrs Lee. I could show her some of the jewellery I've made."

"I'd love that," said Abi, her eyes lighting up. "Can I, Aunty Helen? Then Antonia can go to Sea Watch and everyone's happy."

Mrs Lee sighed. "Well, if you're sure you really want to," she said. "I'll pop in and check it's all right with your mum first, Sophie."

Mum took ages. By the time she came back to the car Antonia's silver dolphin charm had started to whistle. Ella and Jess were giggling together. Even though only a Silver Dolphin could hear the dolphin's call, Antonia was still nervous about the noise. She pretended to rub a crick in her neck so she could cover the charm with her hand. It muffled the sound a little. Then the whispering started in her head. It grew louder until Antonia recognised both

Cai and Hannah's voices answering Spirit's call. Silently she added her own response.

Spirit, I hear you.

"Can I go to Sea Watch now?" she asked as Mum pulled open the car door.

Mrs Lee tutted. "Yes, you can, but don't be long. I want you home for tea."

"Thanks, Mum," said Antonia, leaning over and kissing her mum on the cheek.

She jogged all the way to Gull Bay. The beach was busy, but Antonia found a quiet spot over by the cliffs. Pulling off her shoes and socks she left them in a neat pile and ran down to the sea. Tiny waves ran up the beach and Antonia leapt over them, splashing deeper into the water. When she was in waist deep, she thrust herself forward and swam.

The water was refreshingly cold and she shivered in delight. At once her legs melded together to kick like a tail. Relieved to be on her way, Antonia dived down and swam underwater so no one would notice her swimming in her clothes.

Spirit's call was coming from the east. Antonia was pleased. She'd not answered the call as quickly as she wanted to, but Cai and Hannah would have much further to swim. With luck she could still beat them. The moment she was clear of Gull Bay she surfaced. Swimming in leaps and arcs she flew through the water, her body shimmering in the sunlight like a real dolphin. After a short while Antonia felt vibrations in the water. She swam towards them, sensing they

were caused by Spirit. The coastline was craggy with piles of rocks tumbling into the sea. Antonia swam on until suddenly she saw a shiny head in the water. It was Spirit. Gleefully Antonia hurried towards him. She'd done it. She'd got there first. This time she wouldn't fail. She would solve the problem before Hannah arrived. But as Antonia grew nearer her hopes plummeted. Two figures were moving around on a tiny stretch of beach. Immediately she recognised them. The one nearest to her was Cai and the other person was Hannah, her striking red hair pulled back in a ponytail.

"Silver Dolphin," whistled Spirit. "Thank you for answering the call."

"It's too late though," said Antonia tersely.

She rubbed her nose against Spirit's, but her eyes were fixed on Hannah and Cai as they paddled into the sea. Hannah was waving something. Antonia screwed up her eyes, but couldn't make out what it was. In silence she trod water. Her heart was hammering in her chest and her face felt hot and prickly.

"Hi," called Hannah, as she swam nearer. "Doesn't this make you cross?"

She waved a thin piece of plastic with four holes in it at Antonia.

"Its one of those yoke things that holds cans of drink together. It was wrapped round a seagull's neck. The poor thing might have been strangled if we hadn't got here in time."

Antonia gave Hannah a suspicious look.

What did she mean by that? She hadn't been that slow to answer the call. Considering the circumstances she'd got there very quickly.

"It's great to see you," added Hannah hastily. "Claudia thought you might take a holiday from Silver Dolphins because your cousins are staying."

"I don't want a holiday," Antonia indignantly exclaimed.

She glared at Hannah. How typical that Hannah should save a bird when she'd failed to. Why couldn't Spirit's call have been for litter-picking?

Cai swam over.

"What's going on? Why aren't you speaking in dolphin?" he clicked.

Hannah and Antonia both stared at Cai in surprise.

"Sorry," clicked Antonia, turning to Spirit to apologise.

There was sadness in Spirit's dark eyes. Antonia caught her breath. Spirit's look made her feel uncomfortable. Then the sea began to churn and Antonia spun round. Three dolphins were swimming their way. The sadness vanished.

"Bubbly," she squeaked, as Star, Dream and Bubbles raced closer.

Chapter Eight

"Silver Dolphins," squeaked Bubbles.

He greeted Antonia first. Enthusiastically she greeted him back, pleased that she was still his favourite.

"Can we play, Dad?" begged Bubbles and Dream when they'd said hello to everyone.

Star clicked a laugh.

"I thought you wanted to come here to help the Silver Dolphins," she said.

"They don't need help any more," said Bubbles.

Spirit laughed too.

"Yes, you can play," he generously clicked. "Your mother and I have things to sort out. We'll see you later."

"Bubbly! Thanks, Dad." Bubbles smacked the water with his tail, soaking everyone. "Let's play Sprat. I'll be 'it'. You get a three-wave head start."

Everyone scattered as Bubbles counted three waves. Antonia dived down to look for somewhere to hide. The green-blue water was crystal clear, but there were several rocks dotted around the seabed. She swam behind a

short fat one, lying flat so her stomach was almost touching the sand. It was a good hiding place and Antonia was annoyed when Hannah suddenly appeared behind her, startling a school of tiny fish. Hannah grinned at Antonia in a conspiratorial way as she lay down beside her. Inwardly Antonia sighed. Why couldn't she go somewhere else? But at least Hannah was good at hiding. She didn't wriggle or keep peeking out to see if Bubbles was coming. She didn't get the giggles either, something that often happened to Antonia when she was hiding with Cai. Hannah lay so still she could have been part of the seabed. Trust her to be good at everything. Antonia's resentment continued to build. Well, she wasn't going to let her win Sprat. The moment Antonia felt vibrations in the water she broke cover and swam away.

"Sprat! I see you," whistled Bubbles, chasing after her.

Hannah broke cover and followed Antonia as she swam towards another rock. Determined not to get beaten, Antonia pulled ahead. Movement on the beach caught her eye. What was that? Sprat forgotten, Antonia changed course and headed for the shore where a kittiwake was staggering around. Drawing closer, Antonia saw it was tangled in a length of twine. Suddenly, Hannah changed direction. She'd spotted the kittiwake too. Antonia swam faster. She'd seen the bird first and was determined to get to it before Hannah. She was conscious that Hannah was

catching her up. Frantically splashing ashore she ran up the beach. Startled, the bird opened its bright yellow beak.

"Kitti-waaak," it shrilled, flapping its wings in alarm. The bird tottered and almost fell over as the twine became more tangled round its body and legs.

What was she thinking? By running so fast Antonia was scaring the bird and making things worse. She stopped dead as the panicking bird tied itself in more knots. Hannah ran past her and, lunging at the kittiwake, caught it as it managed to flap a few centimetres off the ground.

"*Kitti-waak!*" squawked the terrified bird, struggling fiercely. A spot of blood appeared on its white breast.

Broken Promises

"Shhh," crooned Hannah.

She held the bird at arm's length until eventually it stopped struggling. Gently, Hannah's fingers worked at untangling the twine. It took ages. Her fingers tugged at the knots until the last piece fell away.

"I'll put this in the bin later," she murmured, putting the twine in the pocket of her shorts. Carefully she examined the bird. Spots of blood stained its white feathers where it had injured itself panicking.

"We can't let it go," said Hannah decisively. "We'll have to take it back to Sea Watch for treatment."

Antonia shook her head.

"Here, let me." She reached out for the bird. Hannah flinched and held on to it. "I said

99

give it here," said Antonia coldly.

Reluctantly Hannah passed the bird to Antonia. She took it, making gentle crooning noises in her throat. The bird fixed her with a steely eye. Gradually it relaxed. Antonia laid three fingers on the wound and imagined it healing.

Mend.

In her mind Antonia saw the wound closing up. A warm feeling crept down her arm and into her fingers. When they began to tingle Antonia pressed more firmly on the wound.

Heal.

The tingling sensation faded, leaving a warm glow that spread into her hands. She held her fingers against the kittiwake for a while longer, then pulled them away. The cut had gone. Only a few spots of dried blood remained. Antonia walked over to the rocks and put the bird down.

"*Kitti-waak*," it peeped gratefully as it flew away.

"Wow!" whispered Hannah. "You can heal. I'd heard that very special Silver Dolphins could. That is so amazing."

Antonia rounded on Hannah, her green-grey eyes blazing.

"That was your fault," she said angrily. "You frightened the bird, charging up the beach like that, and it injured itself."

"I thought it was an emergency," said Hannah. "You were racing too."

"No, I wasn't."

"You were."

Antonia was so worked up she felt dizzy in the head. "I could have managed on my own," she yelled. "I never asked for your help. Or did you think I was going to mess up again? Is that why you came after me?"

Hannah gasped. "Of course not! I was only trying to help. That's what Silver Dolphins do. We work together to care for the sea life, don't we?"

"What's going on?" Cai ran up the beach. "Why are you shouting at each other?"

"She started it," said Antonia. Impatiently she pushed her long blonde hair back over her shoulders.

Hannah said nothing, but her piercing grey eyes were full of concern. Antonia stared at the sand. She didn't want Hannah's sympathy.

"I've had enough of this," she muttered. "I'm going home."

She strode down the beach and into the sea.

"Antonia," called Cai. "Antonia, wait."

Pretending not to hear Antonia waded into the water and swam away. Bubbles and Dream were hovering further out to sea and came after her.

"Silver Dolphin," Bubbles clicked. "Why are you angry?"

"I'm not angry with you," said Antonia, her voice catching. She swallowed. "I have to go. I promised Mum I'd be back for tea."

Dream nuzzled her hair with her nose. "We'll swim with you," she offered.

"Thanks, but I'll be fine," said Antonia.

"You might as well stay and finish your game."

Playfully Bubbles smacked the water with a flipper. "It'll be no fun without you," he clicked. "Please stay."

"I can't," Antonia turned away, unable to bear Bubbles's look of disappointment. "I'm sorry, Bubbles. I have to go home and play with my cousins. I'll play with you next time."

Deep down, Antonia knew she'd acted unreasonably. Why had she felt the need to prove herself to Hannah? Being a Silver Dolphin wasn't a competition. As she swam for home she heard Cai shouting her name. A mixture of emotions buzzed round her head. One was stronger than the rest. She was letting everyone down. She'd even ignored

Claudia's advice to take a holiday from Sea
Watch and from the Silver Dolphins. Antonia
was ashamed of herself. Unable to face Cai,
she swam faster.

Chapter Nine

That evening, Antonia half expected Cai to call to ask if she was all right. Each time the telephone rang she jumped a mile, then was disappointed when the call was for someone else. She thought about phoning Cai, only she didn't know what to say to him. The following day, Mum offered to take the girls out, to visit a tropical garden. Abi, Ella and Jessica were pleased. Not only did the gardens have a huge adventure playground, but there were lots of workshops going on, including one on making jewellery from nature. Antonia wasn't so thrilled about the trip, but remembering her promise to be a good host, she pretended to be excited.

Abi enjoyed the visit to the tropical gardens tremendously but she kept talking about Sophie.

"Sophie would love this," she said, as she sat at an outside table making a bracelet from sunflower seeds. "I'm going to make her a bracelet to match mine."

Antonia wished she'd suggested that Sophie had gone to the gardens in her place.

Then she could have spent the day at Sea Watch and put things right with Cai. Remembering how she'd swum home, ignoring his shouts, made her feel hot with shame. Antonia wanted to prove that she was a good Silver Dolphin. So far she'd only managed to prove the opposite! The day dragged on. Antonia longed for it to end. Tomorrow, Saturday, was the day of the Sea Watch litter-picking event. Now that was exciting! Claudia had said that over a million seabirds in the world died every year as a result of injuries caused by litter. It was a shocking thought. Hopefully lots of people would come to the litter-pick and the sea life would be safer as a result.

The litter-picking event was to be followed

by a huge barbecue on the beach. Claudia
had special permission from Jack to hold one
as a thank you to the volunteers. Antonia
knew Abi wouldn't be keen on the litter-pick
but thought she'd help out so she could go to
the barbecue afterwards. She was wrong.

"Eeeyuk, I'm not spending a day picking up
rubbish," squealed Abi when Antonia
mentioned it. She shuddered, almost pricking
herself with the needle as she continued
stringing sunflower seeds together.

"Please," Antonia begged. "You don't have
to touch anything. Everyone who helps is
given a free pair of gloves."

"Free gloves!" exclaimed Abi. "And that's
supposed to make me say yes?"

"There's a barbecue afterwards."

"I can go to a barbecue any time."

Frustrated, Antonia speared a sunflower seed and accidentally sent it spinning across the table. Ages ago, she'd promised Claudia she'd help at the Sea Watch litter-picking event. More recently she'd promised Mum she'd look after Abi. How could she possibly keep both promises? The summer holidays were rapidly turning into a nightmare.

Luckily Mum came to her rescue.

"Abi doesn't have to do the litter-pick if she doesn't want to," she said. "I'm sure she won't mind if you go, seeing as you've had this arranged for a while."

Antonia could have hugged her mother.

"Thanks," she said gratefully.

"What about me?" asked Abi. "What will I do?"

"You can invite Sophie round," said Mrs Lee. "We'll phone her when we get home."

Saturday morning, the day of the litter-pick, Antonia woke early. Jumping out of bed she ran to her window and opened the blind. The weather was perfect – golden sunshine in a clear blue sky with a sprinkling of fleecy white clouds. The litter-pick was due to start at eleven, but by half past ten so many people had gathered on the beach to help that Claudia ran out of the litter-picking packs. Sally, an adult volunteer, offered to go back to Sea Watch to make up some more and Cai and Antonia went with her to help. Although it was nice having Cai to herself for a change, Antonia felt slightly awkward in his company.

Cai hadn't mentioned the shouting incident on the beach, but occasionally she caught a look in his eye, and knew he was thinking about it. Knowing she couldn't ignore the issue forever Antonia steeled herself to talk.

"Where's Hannah today?" she asked, her hands trembling slightly as she parcelled up gloves, juice and biscuits with a black sack and a green one.

"She's not coming," said Cai. "Her mum felt guilty about abandoning her all week so she's taking her out for the day."

"Oh!"

Antonia was relieved and disappointed at the same time.

They had almost finished. Sally gathered up some rubbish and took it outside. Antonia

112

was about to speak, but Cai beat her to it.

"Hannah's really nice. She'd love to be friends with you. You should give her another chance."

Antonia's green-grey eyes widened.

"You've been talking about me!" she exclaimed.

"Nice things," said Cai.

"Thanks a bunch." Antonia began to put the litter-picking packs into a cardboard box. Nice things or not, she didn't want Hannah having cosy chats about her with her best friend.

"You're so—" Cai didn't get to finish.

Sally came back in jangling her car keys. "Right, let's get this lot back to the beach before our volunteers get bored of waiting and

find something else to do."

I'm so what? Antonia wondered as she helped to load Sally's car.

The litter-pick was great fun and a massive success. Claudia had to arrange for a lorry to collect the bags of rubbish as there were too many to dispose of by herself. A local news reporter and photographer also came along to cover the event for the *Sandy Bay Times*. Antonia and Cai had their photo taken holding up some of the rubbish they'd collected.

"Look miserable," instructed the photographer. "Make it look like you're not happy about finding all this junk on the beach."

No problem there, thought Antonia. Being miserable came easily these days.

In the late afternoon, as the volunteers rested, Claudia and Jack lit the barbecue. Antonia sat on the beach digging up the white-gold sand with her bare toes.

"I wish I'd brought my swimming costume," she sighed. "I'd love to go swimming now."

"Hannah and I are surfing tomorrow afternoon," said Cai. "We might swim after that. Do you want to come with us?"

Antonia was stabbed with a feeling of jealousy. What other things had Cai and Hannah arranged without telling her?

"I didn't ask you before because of Abi," Cai quickly added.

Antonia forced a smile. It wasn't Cai's fault that Abi didn't enjoy the kind of things she and Cai enjoyed. And it wasn't fair to expect

Cai to stay at home doing nothing when she wasn't around.

"Thanks. I might come. It depends on what Abi wants to do."

In her heart, Antonia knew that Abi wouldn't want to spend Sunday swimming and surfing, but she thought her cousin might agree to go to the beach with them to sunbathe. Abi, however, had made plans of her own. The moment Antonia got in from the barbecue, Abi waylaid her.

"We're going to the cinema tomorrow with Sophie. It's all arranged. Aunty Helen said she'd run us into town and Sophie's mum is bringing us back home."

"The cinema!" exclaimed Antonia. "But it's far too nice to go to the cinema. It's going to be hot again tomorrow."

Abi pouted. "Don't come then. We'll go on our own."

Antonia was tempted to say she wouldn't go, but Abi was her guest and she'd promised to look after her. Her cousins were staying for a week. Silently, Antonia counted up the days in her head. It was over halfway through their visit. The three days left seemed a lifetime to go, but it wasn't really. Antonia felt guilty about wanting Abi to go home, but she couldn't help herself. After all, it was Abi that had changed, not her! Suddenly, Antonia was very glad the litter-picking event had happened. With the amount of rubbish collected there had to be less work for the Silver Dolphins to do. With luck Spirit

wouldn't need her until after Abi had gone. That night Antonia went to bed feeling slightly more relaxed.

Chapter Ten

The Sandy Bay cinema was ancient with only one screen and no air-conditioning. It was hot and stuffy and, although the film was funny, Antonia wasn't in the mood for being indoors. At least Abi was enjoying herself. She sat in between Sophie and Antonia holding the huge bucket of popcorn

the girls had bought between them. She laughed so much during the film she reminded Antonia of the old Abi. Furtively Antonia checked her watch. Surely the film was nearly over? Sophie's mum had said to ring them when they got out and she would come and pick them up. Antonia wished they'd asked to walk home. She couldn't bear being cooped up and wanted to be out in the fresh air and sunshine.

A funny feeling swept over her. At first Antonia thought she felt odd because it was so stuffy in the cinema. The feeling persisted. Suddenly, Antonia sat bolt upright in her chair. Of course! Spirit was about to call. Her hand flew to her silver dolphin charm. Its soft body quivered against her fingers. Antonia groaned. Why now? How could she answer Spirit's call when she was at the cinema with Abi and Sophie?

Claudia's words came back to her in a rush. She had said that Antonia could take a holiday from the Silver Dolphins. Reluctantly, Antonia let go of her dolphin charm. She wanted to answer the call, but she also wanted to keep her promise to Mum. Antonia decided that this time she had to let Cai and Hannah deal with it on their own.

A few minutes later, the dolphin charm began to vibrate and an ear-splitting whistle sounded in the cinema. Antonia jumped, guiltily looking around, even though she knew no one else could hear it. The whistling was followed by whispers inside her head. First

Cai's voice and then Hannah's, answering Spirit's call. Antonia longed to join them. But Cai and Hannah were perfectly able to manage on their own. They'd proved that already. Protectively she cupped her hand round the silver dolphin charm. After a long while the whistling ended, but the dolphin charm continued to judder. Antonia felt uneasy. Her sixth sense was telling her that this call was urgent. Should she answer it after all? Whatever she did, it would be wrong. Answering the call meant breaking her promise to Mum. Not answering it meant breaking her promise to Spirit.

The lady next to Antonia began to shuffle. Around the cinema came the noise of seats flipping up and people talking. The lights went on. Antonia wanted to cheer with relief. The film had finished. Abi crushed the empty carton of popcorn with her hands.

"We're going to ring Mrs Hastings and ask if she can pick us up later. Sophie wants to show me a shop that sells handmade jewellery. Is that all right?" she asked.

Sophie looked sheepishly at Antonia. "You don't have to come if you want to do something else," she said.

Antonia shot her a grateful look. Trust Sophie to know she wouldn't want to go to the shops. "Well, I'd really like to go to Sea Watch and check on Tilly the seal. If you're sure you don't mind?"

Sophie grinned. "Of course we don't mind. You and your animals!"

Antonia waited with Sophie and Abi until they'd rung Mrs Hastings and got permission to stay out later. At last she was free to go and she ran all the way to Sandy Bay beach. As she'd expected it was packed with holiday-makers. Antonia threaded her way through them until she reached the rocks. Her dolphin charm was frantically vibrating and every now and then gave out shrill whistles. Anxiously discarding her shoes, Antonia hopped over the rocks to the sea. The cool water lapped at her legs and when it reached her thighs, she swam. Antonia was in too much of a hurry to get her normal thrill of pleasure as her legs melded together. Diving underwater so no one would notice her, she headed out to sea.

The call was coming from the west. Using her dolphin magic to swim even faster than a real dolphin, Antonia struck out towards it. She passed Claudia's beach, and still there was no sign of Spirit. She swam faster, worried that she might not get there in time. She swam for ages. A very long while later, her skin began to tingle with vibrations in the water. Relieved, Antonia altered her course, swimming towards a gap in the coastline where the vibrations were coming from. It was the entrance to a creek. Nearby a silver head bobbed in the water.

"Silver Dolphin," clicked Spirit. "Thank goodness you're here."

"What's happened?" clicked Antonia, knowing that it must be urgent for Spirit not

to greet her with a friendly nose rub.

"Two dolphins are in trouble. They urgently need help."

"Are they from your pod?" asked Antonia.

Spirit shook his head.

"They're strangers. The tide is turning and soon the creek will be too shallow to swim in. It's not safe for me to come with you, so I'll wait here. Go quickly, Silver Dolphin."

Antonia headed up the creek. It was hard to imagine there was a drama ahead of her when it was so peaceful. Trees grew on either side, casting long shadows on the water. Hidden birds serenaded her as she swam. Gradually the creek twisted to the left. The current was stronger here as the water flowed away to the sea. Antonia was forced to swim in the middle of the creek where the water was deeper. As she swam, her senses told her that something bad was ahead. Her stomach churned uneasily. She heard a shout, it sounded like Cai. She sped up and, rounding the corner, she caught her breath. Nothing could have prepared her for this. Dismayed not to have answered the call quicker, Antonia rushed to help.

Chapter Eleven

The creek ended in a tiny beach surrounded by woods. The tide was turning quickly, leaving a large expanse of ribbed sand. It was incredibly pretty and very private, but the peace was spoilt by Cai and Hannah. They were charging up and down the beach, running between the water and two inert forms lying on the glistening sand.

Antonia had never seen beached dolphins before. It was a shocking sight, almost paralysing her with fear. Her dolphin charm flicked impatiently against her neck, urging her to do something quickly. Antonia splashed out of the water and ran towards Hannah and Cai.

"We need to keep them wet," panted Cai. His chest was bare and he carried a dripping wet T-shirt.

Wordlessly, Antonia followed him as he ran to the smaller dolphin and squeezed water from the T-shirt on to its silver-blue body. It was a bottlenose one, its head and nose more rounded than Spirit's, who was a common dolphin. Hannah had a cardigan and was

using that to wet the larger dolphin. Antonia watched them for a minute. She wasn't wearing any clothing that she could remove. But even if she had, she knew that it wouldn't be enough. They had to get the dolphins back into the sea.

When every last drop of water had been squeezed out of the T-shirt, Cai set off again. Antonia grabbed him by the arm.

"Wait, we have to get them back in the water."

"We've tried," said Cai. "We can't shift them."

"But there's three of us now," said Antonia.

Cai eyed her doubtfully. "We need blankets," he said. "I saw beached dolphins on the telly once. The rescuers used wet blankets to carry them back to the sea. It stops their skin from getting damaged."

He shook her arm off and ran back down the beach. Antonia squatted to examine the smaller dolphin. It stared back at her with dull eyes.

"Don't worry. We're going to help you," she clicked.

Feebly, the dolphin flicked its flipper. Antonia slid both hands under the dolphin and tried lifting it. Its body felt like a solid weight in her hands and reluctantly she admitted that Cai was right. The dolphins would be too heavy to carry unless they used blankets to make a stretcher. The only thing they could do was to keep them wet until the tide came back in again and refloated them.

But that would be hours. Antonia knew the dolphins wouldn't survive that long out of water.

"Antonia, help us," shouted Cai, as he came back with a newly soaked T-shirt.

Antonia jumped up and ran along the beach, hoping to find something to carry water in. She ran round twice, her eyes scanning every millimetre of sand, but there was nothing useful. In a panic, she ran to the sea and scooped up water in her hands. It trickled through her fingers. By the time she reached the dolphins, the water was all gone.

The two dolphins lay very still, their dorsal fins pointing upwards like flags. Antonia crouched between them with one hand on each dolphin. Could she use her special healing powers to save them? Was it possible to keep them alive until the tide turned again? Pressing her hands more firmly against each dolphin, Antonia imagined their skin staying cool and moist.

Be strong, she thought. A warm feeling spread down Antonia's hands and her fingers began to prickle. Excitedly, Antonia continued to press on the dolphins' soft skin.

Be strong.

There was barely any response from the large dolphin, but a muscle began to twitch in the smaller one's side. Encouraged, Antonia continued to press on both dolphins until the prickling sensation calmed and a warm glow spread through her hands. The smaller dolphin opened its mouth and let out a high-pitched whistle.

"Help!"

She was calling to her friends.

Suddenly, Antonia had a brilliant idea. She would call a friend to help too. Clearing part of her mind, she concentrated on Claudia, imagining her smiling sea-green eyes staring out from under her unruly mop of hair.

Claudia, we need you.

At first there was nothing. Disappointed, Antonia tried again.

Claudia?

She willed Claudia to hear her and almost cheered out loud when she did.

Silver Dolphin? What's wrong?

Two dolphins are stranded in a creek. We need help to get them back in the water.

I'll be there.

Antonia breathed a heartfelt sigh of relief. It was going to be all right. Claudia was on her way. She started to relax, then an alarming thought crossed her mind. How would Claudia know where to come?

Silver Dolphin?

Antonia jumped. Claudia was still listening to her thoughts!

Keep thinking of me, so I can find you.

I will.

Cai and Hannah pounded up the beach and dripped water over the two dolphins. The smaller was still whistling for help. Cai shot Antonia an excited look.

"Did you do that? Did you make her better?"

"I'm helping them to stay strong while

they're out of the water. I just hope I can keep them alive until Claudia gets here."

"Aunty Claudia's coming? But how..." Cai was puzzled. Then suddenly working it out, his face lit up.

"I *knew* there was something special between you two. I've suspected it for ages. Thank goodness for that."

He pounded back to the sea with renewed energy. Antonia kept her hands on both dolphins, willing them to stay alive. It was exhausting. She was concentrating so hard she almost didn't realise that her dolphin charm had started to thrash again. A lump formed in Antonia's throat and she swallowed it down. She was doing her best. Why was Spirit calling her? Didn't he realise how hard she was trying to keep the dolphins alive? What more could she do?

Hannah and Cai ran up. Side by side, they dripped water on to the dolphins. Cai turned to go back to the sea then stopped.

"Oh no!" he cried. "Spirit's calling us again."

"What now?" groaned Hannah, her hand flying to her own silver dolphin charm. "Surely it can wait?"

"Yes," Cai nodded. "It'll just have to wait. We can't leave these dolphins here on the beach."

Ignoring their whistling charms, they continued wetting the stranded dolphins until suddenly there was a huge commotion in the creek. Surprised, everyone stopped for a moment to look.

"No!" gasped Antonia. "Please, let me be dreaming."

But it wasn't a dream. A pod of bottlenose dolphins suddenly swam into view. They were heading for the beach, drawn by the calls of the stranded dolphin. Spirit swam amongst the dolphins, trying to turn them back with desperate whistles and squeaks.

"We have to stop them," Antonia cried.

She noticed one or two of the dolphins trying to turn back, but there wasn't enough room to swim a different way to the pod. It caused the dolphins to panic, adding to the confusion and noise. Antonia had no idea what to do. Should she stay with the beached dolphins? Or should she try and save the others before they beached themselves too?

It was Hannah who took control.

"You stay here," she said to Antonia. "You're needed to keep these two alive. Cai, you stay too. Help to keep them wet. I'll turn the dolphins back."

She ran down the beach, her red hair flying out behind her. Suddenly, Antonia felt very grateful to Hannah. How would they have managed without her?

"That's a huge task," said Cai, watching her go. "I'll have to help if she can't manage on her own."

"Of course," said Antonia. She remembered what Hannah had said before about working together. "We work as a team."

Cai continued to run up and down the beach using his T-shirt and Hannah's

cardigan to wet the dolphins. Antonia sat between them with her hands pressed firmly against their sides. She was desperate to know how Hannah was doing, but needed to concentrate on her own job. Antonia was concerned about the larger dolphin; he didn't seem to be responding to her magical skills. She hoped Claudia would get there soon. They were running out of time.

Chapter Twelve

Hannah did her best, but she was no match for all the dolphins trying to swim up the creek. Eventually, Cai was forced to abandon his own job and wade into the sea to help her. With outstretched arms, he herded the dolphins back the way they had come. For ages the water was alive with thrashing tails

and fins as the dolphins suddenly realised the danger they were in. Their distressed clicks and shrieks made Antonia's skin prickle with goosebumps.

"Please," she clicked to the dolphin on the beach. "Please, stop calling your friends. The Silver Dolphins are here to help you. Tell your friends to go back to the sea."

The little dolphin fell silent, but it was far too late. Miserably, Antonia wondered why she hadn't thought to ask her to stop calling earlier. And where was Claudia? The Silver Dolphins needed her right now.

Claudia, where are you?

Here.

Antonia looked up and her heart leapt. Claudia was running down the beach towards her, carrying an armful of sheets and a huge watering can. She ran straight past Antonia and dumped the sheets in the sea. Antonia went to help. Together they soaked the sheets in water then draped them over the beached dolphins.

Claudia filled up the watering can.

"Go help the others. I can manage here for a bit."

Antonia's hands were still tingling from using her special dolphin magic. She felt like she'd been for a marathon run. But the drama wasn't over. She couldn't give in to tiredness yet. With a burst of energy, she splashed into the sea to help Hannah and Cai. It was an easier task with three of them. Using outstretched arms they formed a human

barricade. Gradually the dolphins began to turn back the way they'd come. The more that turned, the easier it was to persuade the others to go back too. One dolphin got stuck on a sandbank near the edge of the creek. Working together, the Silver Dolphins managed to free him and guide him towards the deeper water.

When the last dolphin was heading the right way down the creek, Antonia remembered Spirit. He was a large animal. Had he made it safely back to sea? She was wondering whether to swim up the creek to check, when his voice sounded in her head.

Silver Dolphin.

Spirit? Thank goodness. Is everyone safe?

The pod has just reached the sea.

And you?

Yes, me too.

Antonia couldn't help it. She grinned with relief.

"What are you smiling about?" asked Cai.

Antonia blushed.

"We did it," she stuttered.

"Not quite," said Cai. "There're still the two on the beach."

Antonia's relief evaporated. Knowing Claudia was looking after the dolphins had lulled her into a false sense of security. The dolphins on the beach were still in danger. They'd been out of water too long already. Time was running out. At once she headed for the shore. Cai and Hannah swam next to her. It was a good feeling; so many Silver Dolphins

together. They waded ashore.

Claudia was watering the dolphins with her can. Her sea-green eyes lit up as they approached. Antonia dropped on to her knees in the sand between the two dolphins. Claudia had been busy. She'd completely wrapped each dolphin in a wet sheet. The smaller dolphin looked more alert than before. Antonia was worried about the larger one, though. He didn't seem to be responding at all. His eyes were dull and he didn't move when she rested a hand on him.

Be strong, she thought, pressing her hands against each dolphin. Warmth rushed through her and her fingers prickled with magic.

Be strong.

The smaller dolphin's side quivered, but

the larger one was ominously still.

"Antonia..." Claudia's voice broke through her thoughts. "It's time to get her back into the sea."

Antonia looked up and saw Cai and Hannah positioned at the little dolphin's head, ready to carry her on the sheet stretcher. They were whispering together. Hannah shot her a look of sympathy. As she took her place at the dolphin's tail, Antonia wondered what they were whispering about. Then Claudia came and stood opposite her.

"On the count of three," said Claudia. "One, two, three, lift."

Gently they lifted the dolphin off the sand and walked her down to the sea. It was a slow process. Antonia shuffled along, willing

everyone to go faster, even though she knew they were doing their best. The tide was even further out now. They squelched across the wet sand until finally they reached the water. Tiny waves ran away from them, the tide sucking them back to the ocean.

"Don't stop," called Claudia. "Go deeper."

They kept on walking, step by agonising step, until finally the water in the middle of the creek came up to their waists. Antonia looked around, wondering if they should have moved the larger dolphin first. The tide was going out so quickly. He would need more water than this to swim in.

"Gently now," said Claudia. "Turn her round so she's facing the right way."

Everyone moved round until the dolphin's

head was facing out to sea.

"Right then. Let her go."

Slowly they lowered the dolphin into the water.

"Drop the sheet," called Claudia.

Antonia released her corner and the sheet sank away from the dolphin. At first the dolphin didn't move. Then she lifted her head as if trying to work out where she was.

"You're safe now," clicked Antonia. "The ocean's that way. Your pod is waiting for you. Off you go."

The dolphin nuzzled Antonia's hand with her nose.

"Thank you, Silver Dolphins," she squeaked.

"Be safe," clicked Antonia.

"Cai, Hannah," said Claudia. "Swim with the dolphin back out to sea. She's still weak. She may need help."

As Cai and Hannah swam away, Antonia turned to Claudia with puzzled eyes.

"What about the other dolphin?" she asked. "Surely we need help with him?"

Claudia shook her head. "I'm sorry, Antonia."

"What?" Antonia was stunned. "You don't mean... he's not dead, is he?"

Tears stinging her eyes, Antonia struck out for the beach. She could barely see where she was going. Angrily she rubbed the tears away, not stopping until she reached the large dolphin lying motionless on the sand. Antonia fell on him, wrapping her arms round his neck, willing him to be alive.

"Antonia," Claudia panted up the beach and gently pulled her away.

"It's my fault," Antonia sobbed. "It's my fault he died."

"No! It's not."

Claudia put an arm round her. "You did everything you could. We all did."

"But my healing magic worked on the smaller one. Why didn't it work on this one too?"

"This dolphin is very old," said Claudia simply. "The shock of becoming beached was too much for him. I expect his heart gave out. You can save animals when their problems have been caused by people, but not nature."

"Was the beaching caused by humans then?" asked Antonia.

"It must have been," said Claudia. "Otherwise Spirit wouldn't have called for you."

"But how? How could someone cause this?"

"They probably didn't realise they had," said Claudia sadly. "I suspect the two bottlenose dolphins were affected by sonar. Boats use it sometimes. The noise is terrible to a dolphin's sensitive ears. It disorientates them. They don't know where they are going and often beach themselves by mistake."

"What now?" asked Antonia, wiping her tear-stained face. "We can't just leave him here."

"My mobile's in the car. I'll ring Jack and ask him to arrange for the dolphin to be taken away."

Antonia looked at Claudia, grateful she was there. Suddenly, she noticed her clothes. They were bone dry, but her hair was damp and much curlier than usual.

"You used dolphin magic in the water," she said, managing a small smile.

Claudia smiled back.

"Once a Silver Dolphin always a Silver Dolphin," she replied.

Chapter Thirteen

Claudia left Antonia on the beach while she went to telephone Jack. "Tell Cai and Hannah I'll drive you home in the car," she said.

Antonia walked down to the beach to wait for them. She made a wide detour around the dead dolphin, keeping her eyes firmly fixed ahead of her.

I didn't even know his name, she thought sadly.

Cai and Hannah were ages. Antonia grew fidgety and was wondering if she should go and look for them when she heard voices. Looking up, she saw them both wading down the middle of the creek. They waved and Antonia waved back.

"Sorry we took so long," called Cai as he drew nearer. "We took Bella right out to sea to join her pod. Everyone wanted to thank us, they'd been frantic with worry."

"Bella," said Antonia. "That's a pretty name."

"The older one was called Comet," said Cai, his eyes sliding past her to the covered form on the beach. Antonia nodded, unable to trust herself to speak.

By the time Cai and Hannah reached Antonia, their clothes were dry again. Hannah squeezed water out of her long red hair.

"Where's Aunty Claudia?" asked Cai, ruffling his own with both hands.

"She's in the car, phoning Jack. She's going to drive us home," Antonia told him.

"Great," said Cai. "I could swim home if I had to, but I'd rather go by car. I'm shattered."

"Me too." Hannah's face was red with exertion. "That was hard work."

Antonia realised she was tired too. It had been a very long afternoon and it wasn't over yet. As Hannah came towards her, Antonia knew there was one more thing left to sort out.

"Hannah?" she said uncertainly.

"You were brilliant, Antonia," said Hannah, speaking first. "You kept Bella alive."

Antonia was surprised. She didn't feel brilliant and she certainly hadn't saved Bella by herself.

"It was teamwork. Look, I'm sorry about before. You were right. Silver Dolphins work together. I... I should have realised that sooner."

Hannah's pale white skin flushed slightly and she gave Antonia a guilty grin.

"It was my fault too. It was kind of scary meeting you and Cai. Like I said, Kathleen hardly ever helps me. I mostly work on my own. Then suddenly, I find myself working with two Silver Dolphins. I wanted to prove

that I was good enough to do the job."

"But..." Antonia was amazed and suddenly very ashamed that she'd felt the need to compete with Hannah. It didn't matter who was the best Silver Dolphin. Doing the job to the best of their ability was far more important.

"I'm sorry, Hannah. I never realised that's how you felt."

They looked at each other for a moment, then Antonia asked hesitantly, "Friends?"

Hannah beamed. "Definitely."

They walked up the beach. Antonia meant to avoid Comet but, quickening their step, Cai and Hannah headed straight for him. At his head they knelt down and Hannah gently pulled back the sheet uncovering his face. She stroked his cheek, then Hannah quickly kissed his nose.

"From Bella," she explained to Antonia, as Cai copied her.

Taking a deep breath, Antonia knelt down and kissed Comet on the nose. It was the least she could do.

They left the creek and drove along the cliff road. Hannah was sitting in the front, staring out of the passenger window at the sea, when suddenly she shouted for Claudia to stop.

"Dolphins," she cried. "Look, down there."

Claudia pulled the car over on to a grass verge and everyone jumped out. Moving along the coastline was a pod of dolphins, their leaping bodies sparkling in the late afternoon sun.

"My binoculars," said Claudia, reaching inside the car and pulling them out of a pocket. She held them to her eyes.

"Bottlenose," she confirmed, passing the binoculars round for everyone to see. They watched the dolphins and when they were out of sight, Cai broke the silence with a contented sigh.

"Wonderful," agreed Claudia. "Without your help that whole pod would have been stranded and quite probably would have died. I'm so proud of you all. My *wonderful* Silver Dolphins."

The ache in Antonia's heart felt less sore as she climbed back into the car. They might not have been able to help Comet, but at least they had saved the rest of the pod.

Claudia drove on to Sandy Bay. The seafront was packed and there was nowhere to park. Claudia let Antonia out of the car, then drove round the block while she raced down on to the beach to collect her shoes. They weren't where she remembered leaving them. Frantically she searched the rocks. Where were they? It was the first time her things had gone missing when she'd left them on the beach. Antonia was annoyed with herself for not hiding them more carefully. At last, she found one shoe upside down in a clump of dried seaweed and the other close by in a rock pool. Her socks were missing and she gave up looking for them. She was already much later than she'd meant to be and wasn't sure how Mum would feel about

her abandoning Abi, even if she had left her with Sophie.

Antonia kept very quiet on the way home in the car. When Claudia pulled up outside her house, her stomach dipped.

Here goes! she thought nervously.

Claudia switched off the car ignition.

"I'll come in with you," she said. "It's been quite an afternoon. I'd like to explain some of it to your parents."

Mrs Lee did look slightly annoyed when she opened the front door.

"There you are at last," she said. "Abi's gone round to Sophie's for tea. You were invited, but it's too late to go now."

"That's my fault," said Claudia pleasantly. "Could I have a word?"

"Yes, of course, come in," said Mrs Lee, opening the door wider for everyone to crowd into the tiny hall. "Antonia, take Cai and..."

"Hannah," said Antonia.

"Take Cai and Hannah into the garden," said Mum.

"Are you in trouble?" asked Hannah, as they filed outside.

"I'm not sure," said Antonia, flopping down on the lawn. "I've broken a few promises since Abi's been here. It's hard trying to keep everyone happy."

"I'm really lucky like that. It's only me and mum, and she works such long hours she doesn't mind if I stay out late."

"Cool," said Antonia.

"Sometimes," said Hannah wistfully.

Antonia picked at the grass. How would she feel if she was Hannah, with no brothers or sisters and a mother who was always at work? It sounded lonely. At times Antonia's family life made things very complicated for her, but she wouldn't want it any other way. Cai started to talk about his mum and dad and soon he was comparing notes with Hannah about whose parents worked the longest hours.

"You know," said Hannah hesitantly. "You could... if you wanted to, that is... you could come and stay with me when I get home. Both of you, of course," she said, waving a hand at Antonia to include her.

"That'd be great," said Cai. "Then we could help you set up your very own Sea Watch."

"Antonia?" asked Hannah cautiously.

"I'd love to," said Antonia. "We might even get to meet Vision."

"Brilliant," said Hannah, her eyes shining. "I'll ask Mum to fix something up. Weekends are best. She usually gets them off."

"Here's Aunty Claudia," said Cai. "It can't be that bad, Antonia, she's smiling."

They scrambled up as Mrs Lee and Claudia walked towards them. Antonia stared at her mother and cheered up immediately. Mum didn't look annoyed any more. She looked proud.

"What an amazing thing you all did today," she said. "Claudia told me about the rescue on the beach and how you also waded into the sea to stop a pod of dolphins from becoming stranded."

Claudia winked so quickly at the Silver Dolphins that Antonia almost missed it. Then taking a deep breath Claudia said, "They were brilliant and I couldn't have done it without them. However, your mum tells me that Abi and Ella have two more days before they go home, Antonia. So I'm banning you from Sea Watch until then. You're not to come back until Wednesday morning."

"Oh!"

How could Claudia do that?

Antonia was about to protest when she realised that Claudia was smiling right at her. Thinking about all the promises she'd broken, Antonia supposed the ban was only fair. Claudia was helping her not get into any more trouble.

"But what about…" she trailed off, remembering her mum was there.

Claudia raised her eyebrows.

"Today was a very unusual day," she said carefully. "It's not often dolphins get stranded on a beach. Your help was invaluable, but I'm sure that we can manage without you for the next couple of days. So please, promise me that you'll stay away until Wednesday?"

"I promise," said Antonia, and this time she knew it was a promise that she would keep.

"Well done," said Claudia. "Right, you two, into the car. It's time we took Hannah home."

Antonia followed them through the side gate to the front of the house and waved until Claudia's car was out of sight. As she let herself back into the garden, a ray of sunlight caught her silver dolphin charm, making it sparkle. Antonia brushed her fingers across its smooth body.

"Spirit," she whispered. "I'm taking a short holiday. It's only for two days, and then I'll be able to answer your call again. I promise."

The dolphin charm, so soft to touch, juddered slightly in her fingers. Antonia grinned to herself. This time Spirit had answered her call.

Silver Dolphins

OUT
NOW!

Antonia and Cai are on holiday in Australia!
Soon they receive a dolphin call for help – but
what dangers lurk in this faraway ocean?
And why are Antonia's powers fading?

HarperCollins *Children's Books*

Read on for a
sneak preview...

A ntonia woke with the sun on her face. It was filtering in from a different direction than she was used to and for a second she couldn't work out where she was. She opened her eyes and saw three leaping dolphins on the wall opposite. Suddenly everything came back in a rush. She was in Australia with Cai!

At once Antonia jumped out of bed and rummaged through her suitcase for shorts and a T-shirt. Finding her washbag, she pulled out a hairbrush and combed the tangles from her long blonde hair.

On her way to the bathroom she bumped into Cai, still in his pyjamas.

"Hi," he yawned sleepily. "Mum's making us brunch."

Antonia's stomach grumbled hungrily, making them both laugh.

"I'll just have a quick wash," she said.

"No hurry," said Cai, yawning again. "Suppose I'd better get dressed."

Cai took ages and eventually Antonia gave up hovering outside his room and went in search of his parents. They were in the kitchen, where Mr Pacific was cutting up a fresh pineapple while Mrs Pacific fried bacon.

"Hi, did you sleep well?"

"Yes, thanks. Can I do anything?" Antonia felt awkward watching Cai's parents doing all the work.

"You could put the plates on the patio table. We're eating outside." Mrs Pacific pointed her spatula in the direction of the plates then expertly flipped the bacon over. It sizzled and spat and Antonia's stomach growled again.

"Hungry?" Mrs Pacific smiled.

"Very," said Antonia, suddenly feeling more relaxed.

She carried the plates outside then leant on the balcony, taking in the view. It was magnificent. The hotel gardens dropped steeply down to the beach about three metres beneath her. The golden sand, dotted with scrubby vegetation and palms, was fringed by crystal blue sea.

Dazzled by its brightness, Antonia screwed up her eyes. It was so hot. Guiltily, she remembered her sun hat and suncream were still somewhere in her suitcase. Mum had made her promise to wear both whenever she went outside.

But before she could fetch them, Cai and his parents came out, carrying trays of food and drink. While Mrs Pacific arranged the food on the table, Mr Pacific erected a sun umbrella. Thankfully it gave plenty of shade so Antonia stopped worrying about suncream and sat down to eat. It was one of the best meals she had ever tasted. There was a fresh tropical fruit salad, club sandwiches bursting with bacon, prawn salad sandwiches and ice-cold mango and orange smoothies.

"We're planning a few trips out," said Mrs Pacific, helping herself to a large bowl of fruit salad. "And there's plenty to do here in the hotel complex. Why don't you spend today exploring? The pools all have lifeguards so you can swim whenever you like."

"Great," said Cai. "I'd love a swim. What about you, Antonia?"

"Yes," said Antonia decisively. It was so hot she could happily spend all day in the pool.

"Sounds fun," said Mr Pacific. "I might swim too. You two go for a wander while we clear up. I'll come and find you later by one of the pools."

"Are you sure? I don't mind helping with the washing up," said Antonia, pushing back her chair. Was it her imagination or did the tail of her dolphin charm twitch just then?

"Thanks, but there's a dishwasher," said Mrs Pacific chuckling. "That was one of my holiday requests! Tonight we're eating in the hotel restaurant. There's an outdoor one overlooking the beach. It's wonderful and has great food."

Antonia couldn't wait to explore. Quickly she went to her room to put on suncream and get her hat. As she rubbed the cream into her arms, the dolphin picture caught her eye. It was a stunning photo. The leaping dolphins reminded

Buy more great Silver Dolphins books from HarperCollins at 10% off recommended retail price. FREE postage and packing in the UK.

Out Now:

Silver Dolphins – The Magic Charm	ISBN: 978-0-00-730968-9
Silver Dolphins – Secret Friends	ISBN: 978-0-00-730969-6
Silver Dolphins – Stolen Treasures	ISBN: 978-0-00-730970-2
Silver Dolphins – Double Danger	ISBN: 978-0-00-730971-9
Silver Dolphins – Broken Promises	ISBN: 978-0-00-730972-6
Silver Dolphins – Moonlight Magic	ISBN: 978-0-00-730973-3

All priced at £4.99

To purchase by Visa/Mastercard/Switch simply call
08707871724 or fax on **08707871725**

To pay by cheque, send a copy of this form with a cheque made payable to
'HarperCollins Publishers' to: Mail Order Dept. (Ref: BOB4),
HarperCollins Publishers, Westerhill Road, Bishopbriggs, G64 2QT,
making sure to include your full name, postal address and phone number.

From time to time HarperCollins may wish to use your personal data
to send you details of other HarperCollins publications and offers.
If you wish to receive information on other HarperCollins publications
and offers please tick this box ☐

her of Bubbles when he did the twister: a full circle standing on the sea on his tail.

Suddenly Antonia had a very strong feeling that the dolphins needed her. She raised a hand to touch her charm, but stopped when she remembered her fingers were covered with sticky suncream. The dolphin charm began to vibrate, softly at first, then more rapidly.

Antonia was so surprised she stood rooted to the spot. Spirit knew she wasn't in Sandy Bay, so who was calling to her? An ear-splitting whistle rang round the room.

Silver Dolphin, we need you.

To be continued...